THE ELIXIR FIXERS

SASHA AND PUCK
AND THE BREW FOR BRAINWASH

BOOK 4

DANIEL NAYERI

ILLUSTRATED BY **ESTRELA LOURENÇO**

Albert Whitman & Company
Chicago, Illinois

Library of Congress Cataloging-in-Publication data is on
file with the publisher.

Text copyright © 2020 by Daniel Nayeri
Illustrations copyright © 2020 by Estrela Lourenço
Front matter and chapter opener illustrations copyright © 2019 by Anneliese Mak

Hardcover edition first published in the United States of America
in 2020 by Albert Whitman & Company
Paperback edition first published in the United States of America
in 2020 by Albert Whitman & Company
ISBN 978-0-8075-7257-3 (paperback)
ISBN 978-0-8075-7256-6 (ebook)

Printed in the United States of America
10 9 8 7 6 5 4 3 2 1 LB 24 23 22 21 20

Design by Ellen Kokontis

For more information about Albert Whitman & Company,
visit our website at www.albertwhitman.com.

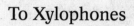
To Xylophones

MAP OF THE VILLAGE

SPARKSTONE MOUNTAINS

SUNDERDOWN FALLS

THE OLD TREE

A MYSTERIOUS PLACE

CATHEDRAL

GENTRY MANSION

SWELTERING RIVER

CAKER

CHOCOLATE SHOP

GRANNY YENTA'S HOUSE

MAYOR'S HOUSE

JEWELER

THISTLEWOOD SWAMP

SHIVERING RIVER

CENTRAL MARKET

GROCER

TINKER CART

THE JUICY GIZZARD

MILLER

VILLAGE SQUARE

VILLAGE GREEN

BAKER

COBBLER

DOCKS

INN

BLACKSMITH

STABLES

STONE LAKE

WHISPERSHAW CASTLE

THE STORY SO FAR...

Sasha Bebbin lives in a village tucked away in a far-off corner of a world, between the mountains and the sea. She lives with her papa in an alchemy shop named the Juicy Gizzard. Her mother was the alchemist, but she has gone off to help fight against the Make Mad Order.

Now, Papa makes and sells the potions. But he's not a very good alchemist.

And Sasha, who doesn't even believe in magic, is worried that customers will start to complain. Then, Papa will be taken to the constable, who will give them a fine that they cannot afford to pay. And then, the wealthy gruel baron, Vadim Gentry, will buy up the Juicy Gizzard, and Sasha and Papa will be homeless.

And so, Sasha has her mission. Along with her sidekick, Puck—a mysterious wild boy from the woods—Sasha must use her detective skills to investigate the real reason every customer wants a potion, whether it's luck or love or just a cure for the hiccups. She has to do this without being discovered. And the hardest part? She has to find a way to make the potion come true, to give the customer the magic they were looking for, before anyone finds out!

CHAPTER 1

Sasha ran as fast as she could through the forest, but it was still not enough. Springtime had come to the Willow Wood. All the flowers bloomed. The butterflies were so big they could have been fairies. Sasha jumped over a tree root to take a shortcut but landed in a puddle of mud. Her boots sank up to the ankles.

"Oh crumbsy bumsy!" said Sasha. She watched as Otto, her disobedient piglet, raced to the foot of a giant hornbeam tree, where they had spotted a precious clump of truffles. "Don't you dare," said Sasha, as she yanked on her foot to free herself. But Otto didn't listen. He ate up the truffles in three bites.

"Gah!" said Sasha. She had spent the entire morning hunting for truffles. Just one would have fetched enough gold at the Village market to pay their bills all season. And that was important because in the springtime, people got all sorts of ideas. Every miller's son would come to the Bebbin family alchemy shop and ask for a love potion, even though everybody knew love potions were the second-most dangerous kind.

And with a stern warning, Papa would sell them.

But it wasn't the dangerous magic that worried Sasha. Sasha didn't even believe in magic. She only believed in science, which meant as far as Sasha was concerned, those millers' sons would be extremely disappointed with their potions.

And that would make them unhappy customers, which meant they would complain, which meant the Bebbins would lose business, which meant they'd lose the shop, which meant they'd lose their home, which would be a disaster! *That* was what worried Sasha. And it was why she much preferred selling truffles over potions.

Sasha shook her fist as Otto chomped on the last of the truffles. "Of all the odds and oddity," she said. "How did we end up with such an unhelpful creature?" Sasha scraped her boots on a mossy stone to remove the mud.

Just then, she felt a cold, wet nose on the back of her left hand. She startled and turned to see Puck crouched on the ground behind her, smiling. If he'd had a tail, it probably would have been wagging. "How many times have I told you not to sneak up on me?" said Sasha.

"Guh," said Puck, who spoke mostly in grunts,

burps, and toots. Puck, as usual, was covered in dirt and tangled hair. Most people in the Village thought he was a dirt fairy or some kind of ogre baby. Nobody knew for sure. But Sasha didn't believe in magical creatures like dirt fairies. She had never seen a fairy, after all. She figured Puck was some kind of wild boy from the Hill Country. Or an orphan from the war.

Puck sat in front of Sasha like a puppy, a wicker basket under his arm. It was Mama Bebbin's foraging basket. Before she'd been called to the war front, Mama had often walked through the Willow Wood, searching for ingredients for her potions and medicines.

"It's all here," she would tell Sasha, waving at the knobby trees and whispering rivers and mossy stones. "All you need to add is knowledge."

As Sasha stood in the middle of the woods, watching Otto eat the precious truffles, she wished once again that Mama would come back soon. Sasha sighed. Her foraging trip had been a bust. "Come on," she said. "Let's go home."

Sasha bent down and picked up the basket Puck had brought. To her surprise, it was as heavy as one of Papa's books. "What's this?" said Sasha.

"Guh, guh!" said Puck, jumping up and down.

"Did you put rocks in the basket?"

Puck shook his head, offended.

Sasha lifted the cover, revealing a treasure trove of forest mushrooms. Fuzzy coral ramarias— perfect for curing diarrhea in people who had it, and causing it for people who didn't. Black trumpet chanterelles, which made a paste that did wonders for the skin. Tree ears for sore throats. Turkey tails for sore bones. And even a few morels, which didn't have any effects but were delicious when cooked in a pan with butter and garlic.

"Amazing!" said Sasha. "Did you...?"

"Guh!" said Puck, jumping in excitement.

"How?"

"Guh!"

"Really? All of them?"

"Guh!"

"That's amazing." Sasha never quite understood Puck's grunty language, but she understood what he meant. And she was thankful that he had gone off on his own to discover all those mushrooms. In the meanwhile, Otto had gobbled up all the sprouts and truffles in sight and was lying on a patch of moss, breathing heavily.

"Welp," said Sasha, "I guess we can go."

She started down the forest path. Puck

scrambled up beside her. Otto would catch up eventually, after a nap.

"Can't wait to show Papa," said Sasha as they crossed a giggling stream and watched tiny river fish playing together. The sunlight glimmered through the branches. Everything seemed happy in the Willow Wood.

Ever since the winter festival, when she'd learned from a traveling knight that her mother was safe, Sasha had found it easier to hope that the war would end soon, and Mama would return for good. All the new leaves and flowers made it feel like the start of a new story—one that wasn't so tense and troublesome.

Sasha was almost skipping as she left the Willow Wood and approached the old alchemy shop where she lived.

"Papa," she said as she opened the back door and entered the house. "Are you here?"

"In the front," said Papa.

Sasha rushed to the front of the store, shouting, "You'll never believe what Puck found! We're all set for the whole season—"

But Sasha was interrupted, and all her joy was ended the moment she entered the room and saw the baron Vadim Gentry and his spoiled daughter, Sisal, standing at the counter with evil smirks on their faces.

CHAPTER 2

Vadim Gentry had more money than anyone in the Village, but it was still not enough. He had schemed for years to take the Juicy Gizzard. He had tried a dozen different plans. Once, he had hired a ratcatcher to set all the Village's extra rats loose in the Bebbins' attic. But Mama had prepared a special soup that made them all fall asleep, and then she'd collected them and released them into the woods.

Sasha stopped short as soon as she saw the Gentrys. And she stopped smiling and started glaring instead. "Hello," she said, because she couldn't help it. Papa had taught her to be polite to all customers, even though Sisal Gentry had once snuck behind Sasha and dipped her hair in a bucket of printer's ink.

Neither Vadim nor Sisal said anything to Sasha.

Papa made a nervous chuckle and said, "Hello, darling. Come in. The Gentrys are just paying us a visit."

Sasha took a step forward. "Can I get you some tea?" she said through gritted teeth. She knew she had to be a good host.

Sisal crossed her arms and curled her lip in disgust. "You'd have to bathe about seven times before we took tea from you." Sisal looked around the shop at all the bottles and herbs and books, as if it were all junk.

Sasha looked down at her clothes and realized

she was a bit dirty from the day's work. She placed the basket of mushrooms on the counter in front of Papa and went to the water basin to wash her hands.

"Where have you been, anyway?" said Sisal.

"In the forest," said Sasha.

"Gross," said Sisal.

"The forest isn't gross."

"Okay, what were you doing in the forest?"

"Digging for mushrooms."

"Gross."

"With Puck."

"That's even worse."

Puck would have lunged at Sisal if Sasha hadn't held him back with her foot. She wiped her hands on a towel and whispered, "She's not worth biting, Puck. And besides, she would only taste rotten."

Sasha took a small cloth out of her satchel

and dampened it
in the washbasin.
Then she returned
to the mushrooms
on the counter and

began to wipe them gently to remove the dirt.

"Did you find anything special?" said Papa.

Sasha nodded. "We found tree ears."

"Is that supposed to be special?" said Sisal. "What does it do?"

Papa and Sasha spoke at the same time. Sasha said, "It cures sore throat," while Papa said, "It cures rainy days."

Sasha glared at Papa. She wished he wouldn't make such claims about magic in front of the Gentrys. They would just *love* to complain to the constable if his potions didn't work.

"I don't care about rainy days," said Sisal as she played with some potion bottles. "I send the servants out to get me things."

Under the counter, Sasha could hear the low rumble of Puck's growling.

"Puck found a bunch of other things," said Sasha, hoping to soothe him. "Even some morels for dinner."

"Ooh," said Sisal. "That sounds good. I'll have that."

Vadim Gentry shrugged and said, "We'll take the morels, then."

Sasha stared at the large man and said, "That's our dinner. It's not for sale."

Sisal rolled her eyes and said, "Whatever. Do you have any potions that make skin shine?"

"Two kinds," said Papa.

"And what about potions to make skin itch?" said Vadim. "Supposing I wanted to make sure my servants weren't so comfortable sitting around all the time?"

"We have itching powders," said Papa, laughing nervously. "But we don't recommend them for use on people."

"Yes, I know," said Vadim. "I said it was for the servants."

Puck was grumbling under the table and snapping his teeth with every word from Vadim. It was obvious to Sasha that the baron wanted some kind of potion. But the mystery was what kind and why. He was acting like he was just browsing, but Sasha suspected he knew exactly what he wanted, and he was just trying to fool Papa by pretending to be curious about alchemy.

As Sisal wandered around the store, the baron leaned one elbow on the counter and asked Papa about the limits of magic. "Can I make a servant stay up all night in order to organize my library?"

And Papa, who loved to explain alchemy, was

falling for it. "I suppose a sleepless syrup would do that, but they'd still be tired from the work."

"And how would you fix that?"

"I'd let them rest."

That answer got a scoff from Vadim. Finally, Sisal chimed in. "What about death potions?"

"You mean to cure death?" said Papa.

"I mean to *cause* death," said Sisal. She seemed to take pleasure in saying awful things.

Papa made a *tsk* sound. "No, no. We can't make death potions."

"Why not? You aren't smart enough?" said Sisal.

"He's smart enough," said Sasha. She realized she had been squeezing a ramaria mushroom so hard she'd almost squished it.

"A death potion is just a bottle of poison," said Papa. "There are poisons everywhere. Nightshade mushrooms, juniper berries, shoe polish, leather wax, perfumes, all kinds of things. It doesn't take any work to find them. What takes work is to make things better in this world."

It was a beautiful idea. Sasha always loved Papa's hope for a better world.

"*Pfft*. Whatever," said Sisal, completely missing the point.

Vadim also seemed to ignore Papa. "What about a potion for persuasion?" he said. "Something to make someone obey all my commands. A mule, for instance."

Papa stroked his mustache. "I could mix that. But it's a dangerous and permanent potion. It will cost four hundred gold."

"Deal," said Vadim. He put a bag of coins on the counter. "Let's have it right now."

That made Sasha even more suspicious. As Papa set to work making the potion, she wondered why the baron had jumped on such an expensive item without even haggling to bring down the price. Out of nowhere, the baron turned to Sasha and said, "On second thought, let's have that tea while we wait."

Sasha couldn't refuse, since she had already offered it. She nodded and began to pour tea from the samovar into tulip-shaped glasses. "Two sugars for me," said Sisal.

Papa mashed a few roots with a mortar and pestle. Then he mixed the paste with the purple oil from an orchid that had come from the other side of the Queen Sea and poured it all into a small bottle. The mixture made an angry sizzle.

Sasha placed four glasses of tea on the counter and one on the floor for Puck. She was startled by a frothy sound. Papa's potion was coming to a boil, even without a fire underneath it.

Papa let out a long, satisfied sigh and took off his goggles. He placed a cork stopper into the round bottle and offered it to Vadim.

"Careful," said Papa. "It's still hot."

Vadim, who was wearing riding gloves, grabbed it without so much as a "thank you." Papa seemed so pleased with the experiment that he didn't notice. Then he remembered something else. "Oh! Right. You must also take this." He pulled out a small glass vial from his pocket and offered it to Vadim. "It's the cure, in case you need to reverse the persuasion potion. Careful with it. They take months to make."

"We won't need it," said Vadim.

"We insist. For any dangerous magic. It's permanent otherwise."

Vadim thought about it, then grabbed the vial.

"Very well," he said as he stuffed it into his coat pocket. "On second thought, I better take it."

Sasha went back to cleaning mushrooms but kept an eye on the Gentrys. Papa started to put away his ingredients. For some reason, the baron and his daughter stuck around. It was unlike them to dawdle.

"It's a wonderful shop you have," said Vadim, as if he and Papa were friends on an evening stroll. It was even more unlike the Gentrys to be friendly.

"Thank you," said Papa.

"Right near the Willow Wood," mused Vadim. "Perfect location for a factory."

"A what?" said Papa. "We would never."

"You could harvest all the plants in the wood and make a fortune."

Papa tried to hide his disgust at the idea by turning around to place a box of silkworms back on a shelf. As soon as his back was turned, the baron quickly uncorked the round bottle and poured half the potion of persuasion into Papa's glass of tea.

Sasha had been scrubbing mushrooms and watching all. She couldn't believe what she had just seen.

Vadim handed the bottle to Sisal, and she poured the other half into Sasha's glass. Sasha wanted to shout, but she was dumbstruck.

She knew the baron was a mean man, but this was true villainy. Before Sasha could speak up, though, Vadim lifted his own glass from the counter and said, "Now, shall we drink to everyone's health?"

"Wait," said Sasha.

"Come on," said Sisal.

"But—"

"Let's be done with it," whispered Papa.

He lifted his glass. Sasha took hers, reluctantly.

"To the Bebbin family," said Vadim, holding his glass in the air to make a toast. "And to the Juicy Gizzard."

Everyone drank.

Everyone except Sasha. She tipped her glass back and poured it into a potted plant behind her.

Vadim smiled. Papa swallowed the entire drink and then took a step back, as if it had made him dizzy. "Hmm," he said. "Did that taste funny to anyone else?"

The baron didn't bother to answer. He simply leaned across the counter to look Papa in the eyes and said, "Now, listen here, Bebbin." The fake courtesy had vanished from his voice and was replaced by a sneer. "I want this shop. And I want it now."

Papa was still holding his head. He said, "Sasha, dear, did we steep the tea too long?"

Before Sasha could speak, the baron interrupted. "I slipped you the potion, you fool."

"I did the same to you," Sisal said to Sasha, laughing. "You're both fools!"

"Now," said Vadim. "I command you to sell me this shop for ten gold."

He slapped a handful of coins onto the counter.

Papa seemed confused. "You want the shop?"

"I just said so," said Vadim.

"You could have killed us, mixing potions with tea like that."

"I was willing to risk it," said Vadim.

"And you didn't let me finish," said Papa. "You don't know how it works."

"Don't tell him!" said Sasha. But Papa was a teacher and an explainer at heart. He wanted, always, to share knowledge. He said, "It's not a potion for making commands. It's for persuasion.

You have to say what you want as a suggestion."

"So I still have to ask?"

Papa nodded. Vadim seemed annoyed that he couldn't simply make demands. "Fine," he said. "Don't you think it would be great if you gave me this shop for ten gold?"

"Of course he doesn't," said Sasha.

"Of course I do," said Papa.

"What?" said Sasha. "No, Papa, don't."

The baron laughed and said, "Oh, but he wants to."

Sasha didn't know what to do as she watched Papa go to the file cabinet and pull out the deed of ownership for the Juicy Gizzard, their family home. With a confused look on his face, Papa offered it to Vadim. The baron snatched it. Then Sisal turned to Sasha and said, "Your turn. I think you should be my maid forever!"

"Of all the odds and oddity, what are you

going on about?" said Sasha. She had no desire to play games with Sisal. But if she didn't, they would think Papa's potion hadn't worked. She was supposed to be under the spell of the potion of persuasion.

Sisal crossed her arms and said, "That's right. You want to be my servant, don't you?"

"Uh, yeah. I mean, yes."

"Good," Vadim said. "Then we're finished here. Now pack your things and be out of here by morning. I have plans for a lovely new factory." He chortled as he turned to go.

Sisal followed. She shouted over her shoulder, "And be at my house tomorrow, ready to polish my shoes." They left the shop and slammed the door behind them.

Sasha and Papa stood completely still in the sudden silence. Puck, who had been watching all this with increasing horror, tilted his head to the sky and let out a howl of despair. Sasha wanted to howl too. But there was nothing she could do in that moment. The Gentrys had won. Papa had given away their shop. They were homeless.

And Sasha was Sisal's servant forever.

CHAPTER 3

"What just happened? I mean, really, Papa, what in the entire world happened? I can't even—I don't even—what *happened*?"

Sasha was panicking. Puck had run off into the woods like a puppy before a thunderstorm. Papa stood in the village market with a wagon cart full of their belongings.

The copper samovar, the mushroom basket, his favorite chair, even Mama's spice cupboard. He was selling everything.

"Everything must go!" he shouted. "All offers

considered."

Sasha paced back and forth behind him, trying to understand the events of the morning. "Did they threaten you before I arrived? Were you scared? Did you lose your mind? What? What could possibly have compelled you to sell the house for ten gold coins?"

"Four hundred and ten gold coins," said Papa. "Don't forget the price of the potion."

"Right. Fine. Okay. But still. Our house! You sold our home."

"Breathe, dear."

"I can't," said Sasha, pacing even faster. "I'm too mad."

Papa sighed and turned away from a customer. He knelt down in Sasha's path and put his hands on her shoulders. Sasha stopped, but her mind continued to race. "Was it the potion? Did it actually work? Is that it? Were you brainwashed?"

She already knew it couldn't have been the potion. She had never seen any of Papa's potions work. It couldn't have been the reason.

Papa shrugged. "A little bit. I did feel dizzy. But it wasn't just the potion."

"Then why did you say yes?!"

Papa sighed again. He reached into his coat and pulled out a ragged piece of parchment. "Here," he said, handing it to Sasha. "It's from your mother."

Sasha grabbed the parchment. It was torn in half, but she could still make out some of the writing. It said:

Desperate
the war is lost
help me
Cover Sasha
—Maxima

"What is this? When did you get it? How? Where?"

"Hold on," said Papa, squeezing her shoulders. "Puck had it a couple days ago. I think he found it in the woods—maybe the letter was lost by the last delivery man. Or maybe a caravan gave it to him. I don't know. He had it in his mouth, and it was already torn to shreds. But it says enough."

"She's in trouble," said Sasha. "We have to help her."

"Exactly," said Papa.

Suddenly, Sasha understood why Papa had sold the shop. He needed the gold to pay for travel. For gear and guides across the Sparkstone Mountains into Rozny. And then, for a horse to cross the Hill Country. And who knew what else? Sasha didn't even know what was beyond the Hill Country. Papa intended to go find Mama, and so he had let himself be tricked by the Gentrys. It all made sense, finally.

Sasha let out a big breath and said, "All right. When do we set off?"

There was a pause.

A long pause.

A pause that made Sasha nervous.

"We don't," said Papa. "I have to go alone."

"Oh crumbsy bumsy, Papa, why?"

"That's all the gold we have."

Sasha felt herself entering a terrible pout.

"Besides," said Papa. "You've got yourself a job at the Gentrys. I was surprised you took it, but it must have been that brew. Even half of it for someone your size—well, it's powerful stuff, you know."

Sasha didn't say anything. Not only had she tossed the drink away instead of drinking it, she didn't even believe in magic. But Sasha knew she had to keep pretending that Sisal's plan had worked, or else it would all be for nothing. The Gentrys would have them arrested for false advertising.

As Sasha considered her predicament, Puck came running up, grunting his most urgent grunt.

"Where have you been?" said Sasha.

"Guh! Guh!"

"That's a vague answer, and you know it," said Sasha.

But Puck had something else on his mind. He

held out a second piece of parchment and said, "Guh!"

"Is that what I think it is?" said Papa.

Sasha recognized it as well. It was the other half of Mama's letter.

Sasha took the piece and put it next to the first to complete the letter. Papa leaned forward to read it with her:

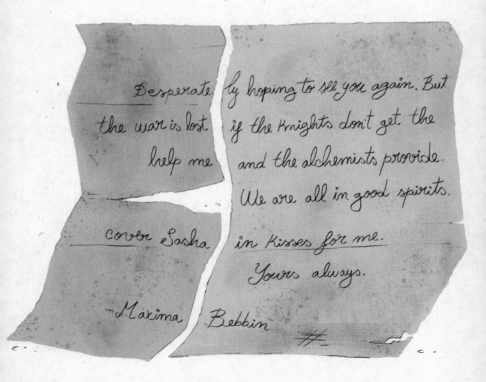

Desperate ly hoping to see you again. But the war is lost if the knights don't get the help me and the alchemists provide. We are all in good spirits.

cover Sasha in kisses for me.
Yours always.

—Maxima Bebbin

"Wait a minute," said Sasha. "Does this mean that Mama is fine, and the war is not lost, and we don't need to rescue her?"

"It's good news, I suppose," said Papa. But he looked so worried that his bushy eyebrows were burrowed into one another.

"Sure," said Sasha, "But now what? Tomorrow morning, we'll be homeless!"

CHAPTER 4

Sasha spent the final night in her own bed unable to sleep.

Early the next morning, just before sunrise, she got up and packed her satchel. The house was mostly empty. Papa had fallen asleep on the floor. He had spent the night hoping to find a solution to their trouble. But they both knew the baron Vadim Gentry wouldn't give back the deed.

Sasha kissed Papa on the forehead. Then she took a pita loaf from beside the oven and packed it with a chunk of sheep's milk cheese, a few slices of fresh cucumber, and a spoonful of honeycomb. She ate it as she walked through the Village in the early dawn light.

The baker's chimney was already puffing smoke. But everything else was still quiet. Sasha passed by the Wander Inn, the blacksmith's workshop, and the village green. Then she crossed the bridge to Upside and passed the bonbon shop. After a while, she felt a little tug on her pant leg. When she looked down, she saw it was Puck.

He was still rubbing his eyes and yawning. He must have woken up and run after her. Sasha didn't have anything to say, so she held out the rest of her breakfast. Puck smiled and took a bite.

"Take it," said Sasha. Puck took the sandwich, and they walked on in silence. Maybe it was the

early morning. Or maybe it was the loss of their house. But neither of them made any noise as they left the Village and walked up the hill, past the stabler's tent. It looked closed. The stabler, Oxiana, must have been away on a journey.

They approached the Gentry mansion. Sasha didn't want to admit it, but she was afraid. As they approached the giant door, she reminded herself, "It's just a persuasion potion, not a command potion. So Sisal has to say stuff in the form of a question, and I just have to pretend to be persuaded."

But for how long? Being "persuaded" by Sisal sounded terrible. No matter how Sasha considered it, this situation was simply the worst.

It wasn't like other cases, where she could solve her problems with her detective skills. Usually, she would investigate what the customer wanted and help them get it. But this time, she

already knew what the Gentrys wanted—the deed to the Juicy Gizzard. And they already had it. And Sisal had turned Sasha into her personal servant. And it was all over and everything was ruined.

The door opened with a sound like a dragon's yawn. The Gentrys' butler stood in the doorway, scowling down at them. Sasha said, "Um, hello, Mr. Butta."

Butta didn't say anything.

"We're here to, uh, visit Sisal."

Butta looked at Sasha, unimpressed, then at Puck, disgusted. "Yes, but why is that ragamuffin here?"

"Who, Puck? He's with me. We work together."

"You work for lady Sisal now. He stays out."

Puck made a rude grunty sound. Butta's lip curled up at Puck's behavior. The butler was unmoved. Sasha knew there was no point in arguing. She pulled Puck aside and knelt down to look him in the eye. "Listen, Puck," she whispered. "I can handle this part."

"Gooby, gooby," said Puck.

"I know. He's probably still mad that you stole all those cookies from his tea party that one time."

"Guh," said Puck, admitting it was true.

"Besides," said Sasha, "I need you for an important mission."

Puck stood up straight. He took great pride in being given important missions.

"If we're going to get out of this, we need help," said Sasha. "Can you go back to the stables and find Oxiana?" Puck loved Oxiana the stabler and often ran errands for her.

"It's a long shot," Sasha continued, "but maybe she knows if there are any messengers going east into the mountains. We'll have to get a letter to Mama if we can. She'll know what to do."

Puck was bouncing and nodding by this point, like a puppy waiting to be thrown a stick. Any mission to do with Mama was an important one indeed, and he was excited to show what he could do. For all his messiness, Puck was a good-hearted helper, and Sasha wished she could keep him with her.

She worried that he would become distracted and wander off. But she had no choice. Butta cleared his throat. He was losing patience. "Okay, go," said Sasha. Puck turned and sprinted down the hill. He had already forgotten Butta's insult.

Now Sasha was truly alone.

She took a breath and decided to be strong, because she still had that choice. "All right, Mr. Butta, it looks like we're coworkers now."

Butta didn't say anything. Sasha followed him into the Gentry mansion. It was a cold, stone manor with a maze of hallways and an army of servants. Sisal's bedroom was at the top of the tallest tower. Sasha climbed its circular marble staircase until she was aching and dizzy.

At the top of the stairs, she stopped to catch her breath. Out of a tiny window, she could see all the Village nestled in the valley, and where the Sweltering River rushed into the Shivering River, and off by itself in the corner, her little house, tucked beside the Willow Wood. Sasha let out a deep and hopeless sigh. It wasn't her house anymore.

Her thoughts were interrupted by a screech.

"Girl?" Who else could it be but Sisal Gentry. "Girl! I know you're out there. I can hear you panting like a hog." Sasha turned away from the window and saw two closed doors in the entryway. Which was the right one?

"Well?" shouted Sisal, "Come in! Here, piggy, piggy." Sasha approached the first of the two doors and opened it. "Wrong!" said the voice. "That's my washroom."

It was true. The washroom had a porcelain vase and a matching washbasin. Towels from beyond the mountains sat on a shelf, as puffy as clouds. Sasha closed the door and tried the other. This one opened into a vaulted, circular room that took Sasha's breath away. It had tall windows with real stained glass made by the Sparkstone monks, and it was filled with shards of multicolored light.

Shelves of toys and books lined the walls

below the windows. Sasha had never seen so many—not even at the holiday market. At the center of the room was a four-poster bed made of wrought iron, piled high with mattresses. At the center of all those mattresses was Sisal Gentry.

"Finally," she said. "You should have been here hours ago."

Sasha didn't say anything.

Sisal waited. Then she said, "Well?"

"Well what?" said Sasha.

"Where's my breakfast?" said Sisal.

"Am I supposed to have it?" said Sasha.

"You are my servant now, girl, so yes, you're supposed to have it."

"My name is Sasha."

"I know. We've known each other forever. But I'm calling you, 'girl.'"

Sasha said, "Well, I don't have your breakfast."

"Don't take that tone with me," said Sisal, sitting up in her bed.

"I don't think you know how potions work," said Sasha. "You can't just demand stuff."

Sisal let out an exasperated breath. "Fine," she said. Then she twisted her face into a mocking, sweet expression and said, "Would you prefer to speak to me like I'm a princess?"

Sasha wished she could spit on the floor and storm out of the room. But it was no use. She had to pretend for now, until she could form some kind of plan. So she jigged her eyebrows and blinked three times, as if some kind of magic was persuading her. Then she said, "Yes, oh honorable and royal highness."

Sisal giggled and clapped her hands. "Much better. Now, *girl*, wouldn't you like me to call you 'girl'?"

Sasha tried not to roll her eyes. "Yes."

"Yes, what?"

"Yes, princess."

"Good. And wouldn't you like to go downstairs and get me two eggs, a wedge of salty cheese, a jar of forest honey, tea—very hot, very strong—a warm loaf of bread, clotted cream, and three tulips in a tall glass?"

Sasha clenched her jaw so she wouldn't say anything rude. Sisal was loving every second of this. "Well?"

"Yes, princess," said Sasha through gritted teeth. She turned to walk out. She had only just caught her breath, and now she had to walk down the tower steps, across the mansion to the kitchens, and back again. Sasha was beginning to think that this would be even harder than she'd thought. But when she entered the kitchens in the basement, she realized it would be even harder than that.

CHAPTER 5

The kitchens were nothing like the kitchens Sasha was used to. Everything was clean and orderly. The walls were white tile. The pots and pans were stacked in perfect rows. Every item was in its place. The cooks were dressed in white uniforms and worked in a line, in complete silence.

Sasha wasn't sure what to do. She stepped into the kitchen, but no one spoke. She made a coughing noise. Still, nobody noticed. Sasha figured she would have to find Sisal's breakfast herself. But where to start? She spotted a stack of pearl-handled trays—one of those would be helpful. She tiptoed past the cooks and took a tray.

From there, she could see a pantry with shelves carved into the stone walls, and little terra-cotta jars lined up by size and shape. That seemed like a good place to start. She searched the handwritten labels on each jar—pickled parsnips, onion paste, mulberry jam—until she found the honey section.

Sasha was amazed by the number of honeys from all sorts of places. Coriander honey from Rozny. Hill Country wildflower honey. Orange blossom honey from the floating gardens beyond the Queen Sea. And there—in the smallest jar— forest honey from the Mad Woods, where the monks of the Make Mad Order lived. Sasha wondered what it tasted like. It must have been impossible to find, ever since the war started.

As she reached for the jar, Sasha was suddenly jolted back to reality by a gruff voice. "Who're you, and what are you doing in my kitchen?"

Sasha whipped around. "Nothing!" she said.

The woman standing behind her was tall and unsmiling, with milk-white hair pulled severely back into a bun on top of her head. She wore a chef's uniform like those of the cooks, but hers was embroidered on the left breast with the Gentry house crest and a floral pattern on the shoulders. Everything about her was sharp, clean, precise. And she was holding a butcher knife.

"Nothing?" said the stern chef. "I suppose we know who you are now."

"Huh? I'm Sasha Bebbin."

"You're a liar, Sasha Bebbin."

Sasha was flummoxed. "No. I wasn't doing anything wrong."

"Lying is wrong, Sasha Bebbin. So is stealing."

"I wasn't," said Sasha, feeling her face flush. "I'm..."

"A liar and a thief."

Sasha felt like Puck in that moment, misunderstood and unable to speak her own defense. Her mother had always taught her, whenever she was frustrated, to stand up straight, breathe, and begin again.

Sasha did just that, and said, "My name is Sasha Bebbin, and I'm the new maid to Sisal Gentry. I was sent here to get her breakfast, which is two eggs, a wedge of salty cheese—"

The chef interrupted her. "This way." She turned and walked across the kitchen. Sasha hurried to keep up. As she passed behind the cooks, Sasha could see them stiffen. The chef continued into a separate room with a stone oven big enough to hold five of Mama's biggest cauldrons. Beside the oven, Sasha spotted a tray filled with all of Sisal's requests. The chef took it and handed it to Sasha. "Did you think my kitchen wouldn't know the mistress's breakfast?"

Sasha stayed silent. It felt like such unfairness to give her so little information and punish her for making guesses. But she bowed her head and said, "I'm sorry, ma'am."

"My name is Barza, but you will call me Chef."

"Yes, Chef."

"When you enter my kitchen, ask one of my cooks for what you need, and they will get it for you."

Sasha flushed again, this time with anger. "I did that! They wouldn't look up."

The chef crossed her arms at the insult to her crew. "Good. They should keep working until a request is made. Did you speak up and announce yourself?"

Sasha wilted. "No. Not exactly."

"Why?"

"I was afraid."

"The truth. Very good. Why were you afraid?"

"They looked busy and mean."

For the first time since meeting Chef Barza, Sasha saw the faintest smile. "That's because they *are* busy and mean. Go. Get this to the little princess."

Sasha rushed out of the kitchens with the tray of food, feeling that she had escaped some sort of dungeon full of deadly traps and dangerous creatures.

★★★

Sisal made Sasha stand beside her bed and watch her eat the entire breakfast. Then she said, "Get

me water. I mean, don't you want to get me water?"

So Sasha had to go back down the tower, then up again, carrying a big sloshy basin full of water. Sisal washed her face and then made Sasha help her get dressed, braid her hair, and scrub her feet, barking out orders in the form of questions until Sasha was exhausted. And it was only teatime.

"This'll be fun, won't it?" said Sisal as they descended the stairs. "I'm going to eat at least three bonbons."

Sasha followed. She had so little time to think,

but somehow, she needed a plan to get that deed back. In her mind, she tried to make a list of possible solutions:

1. Discover the location of the deed and sneak away with it.
2. Offer Vadim Gentry something that he wants more than their house.

On top of that, she would need to find some way to make everyone believe that she had reversed the persuasion potion—so she and Papa wouldn't have to obey the Gentrys anymore. It all sounded so impossible.

Sasha tried not to cry as they walked into a parlor big enough to hold Sasha's whole house. It was full of beautiful furniture. The walls of windows overlooked the gardens.

Butta—the head butler—stood at the main entrance, directing his staff as they set out

flowers and played music. Barza—the head chef—
stood beside the door to the servants' halls,
watching her cooks as they set out trays of
baklava, almond cakes drizzled with cherry
syrup, cream puffs, and a bejeweled samovar of
hot black tea. It only took Sasha a second to
realize that Butta and Barza must be twins. They
were exactly alike—tall, thin, severe.

At the center table sat Vadim Gentry. In front of him was a riveted oak box full of papers and mail. The baron was reading a letter as Sisal approached and said, "Hi, Daddy," and kissed his cheek. The baron patted her on the head without looking up. Sisal took her seat and said, "Hello, Mother." Sisal's mother, Rose Gentry, sat on the other side of the table. She had her own chair, which the servants used to roll her from room to room. She sat holding a glass of tea, with a peaceful smile on her face.

There was one other chair at the table, for Basil, Sisal's older brother, who was away on a painting trip to Rozny. Sasha wished he were there, more than anything. Basil had a good heart and would have probably helped her. But no such luck. Sasha was alone.

Sasha stood to the side as Sisal dove onto the cakes. Sasha tried to inch her way along the wall to get a look inside the baron's strongbox. Maybe the deed to the house was in there? She craned her neck and stood on tiptoes until the baron noticed her. He didn't say anything and kept reading. But he reached up and snapped the wooden box shut. Sasha retreated back to the wall, where Butta gave her a disapproving *tsk* sound.

The sound seemed to knock Mrs. Gentry out of a daydream. When she noticed Sasha, she said, "Oh, hello, dear."

Sasha raised her hand to give a silent wave.

"Mother," said Sisal. "Don't speak to her. She's just the help now."

Rose Gentry smiled and ignored her daughter. "Tell me. How are you?"

"Not very well, ma'am," said Sasha.

"Yes, I was sorry to hear." Rose's smile faded for the first time as she cast a glance at her husband. "And how is Maxima?" said Rose. The sound of Sasha's mother's name made her jump. The question pulled Vadim away from his papers and Sisal from her cakes.

"Mother," said Sisal.

"Rose," said Vadim. "You shouldn't agitate yourself in your condition."

"I'm fine," said Rose. She looked back at

Sasha. "Have you heard any news?"

Sasha squirmed as all the eyes in the room turned to her, glaring. All except Rose's. She seemed genuinely curious. "We've heard a little," said Sasha. "She's stationed with the Knights of Daytime. Her medicines save lives."

"She's doing very important work," said Rose. "We were best friends, you know."

"Really?" said Sasha, stepping forward.

Rose nodded. "Her tea worked wonders for my joints. We had you and Sisal in the same winter storm. And before that, we attended Sunderdown Academy together. She studied alchemy and cures while I studied dance, but we were sisters for a while. She had your spark. I'm sure you have her knack for solving problems."

Rose gave Sasha a gentle wink.

Sasha felt her heart swell and tears well up in her eyes.

It had been such a hard few days, and to hear about her mother made her feel less alone. Sisal was not amused, however. She chewed up a cookie as if she were punishing it. As Sasha opened her mouth to say "thank you" to Mrs. Gentry, Sisal broke in. "Sasha, wouldn't you rather stop talking, get out of my face, and go help Barza shop for groceries?"

Sasha closed her mouth, lowered her head, and walked out.

CHAPTER 6

Sasha waited outside the Gentry mansion, holding back tears and kicking rocks. Barza had work to finish in the kitchen before she could go to the market. It was raining a warm spring rain. Sasha let it soak her hair and her clothes. She tried her best to enjoy the short break from chores.

Her papa always said that "Hope is the best use of courage." But hope felt almost impossible.

Just as Sasha was wallowing in her problems, she heard a rustling from the hedgerow. It could have been Abrus, the Gentry guard dog, which was more of a guard wolf. Sasha braced herself. But the creature that emerged was Puck. The rain hadn't managed to clean him. The soot and dirt that constantly covered him had just turned to mud. But for once, Sasha didn't care. "Oh, Puck! What are you doing here? If they see you, they'll set Abrus on you."

Puck stumbled up to her and plopped onto the ground. He was panting as if he'd been running nonstop. "Are you okay?" said Sasha. She had never seen him this tired before.

He didn't answer. He reached into his pocket and pulled out a crumpled wad of wet and muddy paper.

As he caught his breath, he held it out to Sasha.

"You expect me to touch that?"

"Ugga mugga," said Puck, rolling his eyes.

"Fine, but you look even worse than usual, Puck."

She took the paper between two fingers and began to unravel it. As she did, she said, "Did you go to the stables?"

Puck nodded yes.

"Did you find Oxiana?"

Yes.

"Can she send a message to Mama with the next caravan?"

Yes.

"And is there a caravan coming?"

Puck shook his head no.

"Great," Sasha said with a sigh.

"Guh!" said Puck, gesturing at the paper.

"All right, all right." Sasha turned to the page

and began to read. *"My dearest Sasha."* She paused. "Is this?"

"Guh!"

Sasha jumped to the bottom of the page. It said, *"With all my love, Maxima Bebbin."* It was. It *was* a letter from her mother. Sasha's mind was racing. She looked at Puck. "But how did you get this? From a messenger?"

Puck shrugged. Sasha returned to the letter:

My dearest Sasha,

It's busy here, and I can't write a long message, but I heard the terrible news from Prince Carvalio. Losing the house and the shop must be devastating. Stay strong, my girl, and take care of Papa. If you need to reach me, just give a note to Prince Carvalio.

With all my love,
Maxima Bebbin

That was it. Sasha could hardly believe that her mother had spoken to her. It felt like she was right there with Sasha. But then the questions began to flood in.

"Where did you get this?"

Puck shrugged.

"From Mama herself?"

Puck nodded.

"So then who's Prince Carvalio?"

Puck sat up straighter and smiled.

"You?"

He nodded.

"Are you really a prince?"

Shrug.

"Is that just what Mama calls you?"

Puck nodded.

"How do you know her?"

Shrug.

"You're no help, you know that? I'm still

calling you Puck," said Sasha.

Puck let himself fall back onto the wet ground and opened his mouth to drink the rain. Sasha thought about it for a moment. Mama was at least twenty days' ride away, over the mountains, past the Hill Country. It was too far. If he'd run, it would have to be so fast that it was magic. Sasha didn't believe in magic, of course. But maybe a wild boy like Puck had eagle friends?

Or maybe Mama was closer than she thought? As Sasha puzzled over the message, she heard footsteps coming from behind the door that led to the kitchens. Puck sat up.

"You have to go," said Sasha, "but can you really get a note to Mama?"

Puck nodded and held out his hand for the note.

"I haven't written it yet, but I will. Find me later."

Puck dove into the hedge, and Sasha stuffed the letter in her pocket just as Barza opened the door. The rain immediately stopped, as if it were scared of Barza too. "Who were you talking to?" demanded Barza.

"No one," said Sasha. "I mean, just a dirt gremlin named Puck, who may be a prince named Carvalio."

Barza blinked one, two, then three times. "I don't enjoy silliness," she said. She turned and began to walk down the hill. She pointed at a pile of baskets by the side door and said, "Bring those." Sasha hurried to pick them up and followed the chef. From the hedge, she could hear Puck giggling.

The walk to the Village wasn't easy.

Sasha had to carry all the baskets and keep up

with Barza, who marched too quickly on rain-slick stones. But even as she struggled, Sasha couldn't stop thinking about Mama's letter. Maybe Mama would show up out of nowhere and solve everything? Maybe she'd bring the Daytime Knights and force Baron Gentry to give back the deed?

"Keep up," shouted Barza.

Sasha snapped out of her childish dreaming. "I was wondering," she said. "Are you and Butta related?"

Barza didn't say anything for a moment. Then she said, "He's my brother."

"It must be nice to have a brother," said Sasha. "I have a friend who is like a little brother, but he makes a lot of trouble too."

"You talk too much," said Barza.

Sasha shrank back into herself. As they entered the village market, she heard Papa's voice.

"Step right up and get yer bone soup! Better than stone soup, and easier to chew. Just two pennies, and you keep the bottle. Step right up."

He was standing in the corner of the market, beside the butcher's cart. In front of him was a cauldron big enough for Sasha to bathe in. He stirred it with an oar and called out to customers wandering the market stalls.

Barza rolled her eyes and made an irritated

snikt sound. Sasha already knew that Chef Barza would never approve of her cooks being so loud. But this was exactly what Sasha needed. She said, "Chef Barza, I could go pick up the bacon if you wanted."

"No," snapped Barza. "Stay beside me."

"Okay," said Sasha. "Then we just need to stop by that butcher to get Sisal's favorite bacon. He's over there by that loud soup peddler."

Barza made a sour face. "Fine," she said. "Go, and find me at the greengrocer afterward."

Sasha nodded. As soon as Barza turned and walked away, Sasha ran up to Papa and said, "Papa, what are you doing, and why?" Then she added, "Please stop immediately."

Papa set down the oar he was using to stir and said, "Hello, my darling girl."

"That's not an answer, Papa."

"I'm selling bone soup, didn't you hear?"

"Yes, the whole Village heard."

"Good. Maybe they'll buy a bottle." Papa picked up a ladle and dipped it into the massive cauldron. He scooped up some soup and poured it into a glass bottle that Sasha recognized. It was one of the potion bottles from the shop.

"I spent the whole morning scavenging ingredients from the lakeshore and the forest," said Papa. "Sorrel, wild carrots, those mushrooms you found. My new butcher friend gave me all the bones he didn't need. I threw it all in the pot. Before I knew it, I had soup." Papa had a chipper tone that made Sasha doubly sad. She knew he was trying to make the best of things.

"It's not all that different from alchemy, actually," he said.

"Oh, Papa, that is terrible alchemy."

Papa nodded. "Well, I wasn't a very good alchemist, I'm afraid."

All her life, Sasha had believed in science, not magic. But still, it was awful to hear Papa doubting himself. "Where did you get the cauldron?" she asked, to change the subject. They had sold theirs already.

"Granny Yenta let me borrow it," said Papa. "She really did us a favor."

Granny Yenta's daily stew was famous around the Village. It was awfully nice of her to let Papa have her spot to make a few coins. Papa seemed proud of his new job, so Sasha tried to be encouraging. "The bottles are a nice touch."

"Aren't they?" said Papa. "It's like a magic soup that will heal all your hunger." He laughed to himself and handed a bottle to Sasha. She took it and put it in her satchel for later.

Sasha had been wondering something ever since she saw her father, and now she just had to ask.

"Papa, where are you going to sleep tonight?"

Papa poured the soup into another bottle and said, "Oh, that's no problem. I'll just wash the cauldron in the river and sleep under it. The beautiful stars in the springtime air will be my blanket. It's going to be great!"

Sasha said, "But can't you use some of the money to sleep at the Wander Inn?" They had plenty of coins from the baron's deal, but Sasha already knew Papa would never use that money on himself. Not when his daughter was a servant in the Gentry mansion.

"I'm fine," said Papa. "How are you holding up?" His smile was gone. He stirred the soup slowly.

"Oh, I'm great," said Sasha. She didn't look him in the eye.

"Do you have a nice room?"

"I think so."

"You think so?"

"Yeah, probably. I haven't had time to check."

Sasha was almost certain that Sisal wouldn't be giving her a room, but there was no reason to make Papa worry. They were both silent for a while. The market was full of people going about their lives, buying vegetables or candles or lamp oil, and maybe none of them knew that Sasha's whole life was in trouble. She sighed. "I got a letter from Mama. Puck delivered it."

"Really?" said Papa.

Sasha nodded.

"Do you think she's close by? We could use her help," said Papa.

"I was thinking that too," said Sasha, but before she could come up with a plan, she felt a hand clamp down on her shoulder.

"What did I tell you?" said Barza.

Sasha whirled around. "Sorry!"

"I waited at the greengrocer until I realized you are an untrained puppy."

Sasha's cheeks flushed. She looked at her shoes because she wasn't used to being scolded. Papa came to her rescue. He put on his best smile and said, "Hello, Chef. May I offer you some soup?" He held out a spoonful of soup.

"Sisal might like some," said Sasha.

Barza took the spoon and sniffled it, then put it in her mouth, then turned her head and spat on the ground.

"Disgusting slop," said Barza. "Fit for dogs, and not even particularly good dogs."

Papa made a nervous laugh. "Okay," he said. "Thank you for your advice."

Barza turned away from Papa without another word and said to Sasha, "Come."

Sasha was filled with shame for her papa's soup and for Barza's rebuke. She waved to Papa quietly and followed Barza out of the market. Maybe these were their lives now—soup peddler and servant to the Gentry house. Maybe nothing would ever get better and everything would stay this bad forever.

CHAPTER 7

By the time she returned to the mansion with Barza, Sasha realized her life wouldn't stay that bad forever. Because it got much, much worse.

"See this?" said Barza, waving at the entire kitchen, including a sink full of pots and pans, ovens splashed and stained with food, a messy pantry, and more dirty dishes than Sasha could count. "Clean it."

"The dishes?" said Sasha.

"All of it. Floor to ceiling. Everything spotless."

Sasha couldn't even imagine how long it would

take. But Barza didn't seem to care, and Sasha didn't have anywhere to go. She knew that if she refused, Sisal would just have to come down and "persuade" her, and she might punish Sasha with even worse chores. So she took the mop and bucket and got to work.

It was gross and grueling work. Sasha scrubbed all through dinner. She scrubbed as the sun set through the tiny window above the dishwashing station, and even after the full moon rose to the top. All the cooks were long gone. All the house was asleep.

Sasha scrubbed the last dish and arched her back to relieve the pain. She looked around the kitchens. Everything was shiny and clean. She thought, *Barza can't possibly complain this time.*

Then she yawned. It was past midnight, and Sasha realized that no one had told her where she should sleep. Sasha wondered if Butta would be awake, or if she could find the servants' quarters. Maybe there would be a bed for her, or a bench, or some corner of a quiet hallway where she could curl up and rest.

Sasha wandered out of the kitchens. The entire floor was empty. When she arrived at the staircase, she paused. The stairs leading back up to the house were dark, but a set of stairs leading down to a second basement glowed with a faint light from somewhere below. Could it be the servants' rooms? Maybe they were all still awake.

Sasha decided to go down the stairs.

Her felt shoes didn't make any noise on the stone steps as she went around and around and down and down.

Sasha started to worry that she had gone the wrong way when finally the stairs ended, letting her out into a long hallway. The light was coming from a door at the far end. Sasha didn't know why, but she decided to stay quiet and tiptoe toward the light. The basement was as cold as a dungeon.

She couldn't hear anything at first, but as she approached the light, she began to hear shuffling sounds, but no talking. That meant it was probably just one person. Suddenly, Sasha doubted that this was the servants' rooms. She was too curious to turn back though.

She held her breath and slowly peeked around the corner, into the room. She nearly gasped when she saw Baron Vadim Gentry standing at a desk. The room had leather seats, a large desk, cabinets, and a weapons rack full of swords in every size and shape. This must be the baron's secret office.

Sasha had always been a terrible spy because she was terrible at being quiet. But she had changed a lot in the last year, and so she calmed herself, slowly breathed in and out, and held still. From the pitch-black hallway, she watched as the baron put some papers into the oak strongbox he'd had at teatime. Then he picked up the box and walked to a framed portrait of Rose Gentry standing on her toes in a dancer's pose, with one arm held above her head and the other holding the reins of a white horse so beautiful that it was probably a bloomhoof stallion.

As Sasha admired the painting, the baron took one corner of the frame and pulled it away from the wall. There was a secret cabinet behind the painting. And to Sasha's amazement, she could see Papa's vial—the cure to the persuasion potion—sitting on the bottom shelf beside a rolled-up parchment, which must have been the deed to the Juicy Gizzard.

Sasha couldn't believe it. She stepped closer to get a better look. But the baron placed the box on the shelf, swung the painting back into place, and turned around too quickly. It caught Sasha by surprise. She jumped back out of the doorway.

"Who's there?" said the baron.

Sasha froze in the dark hallway. She hoped the baron would go back to his work. But just in case, she began to tiptoe slowly back down the hall. It was good that she did.

The baron was a suspicious man. A few moments later, a lamp was thrust into the hallway, and the baron stuck his head out the door. "If you're down here, you had better beware the dog."

Sasha had already snuck out of the light's reach and hid in another doorway. She didn't want anything to do with the guard dog, Abrus. She moved as quickly and quietly as she could, and she didn't breathe until she reached the stairs and rushed back up to the kitchens.

Sasha had nowhere to go or sleep.

She was exhausted from work, terrified of the baron and his dog, and worried for Papa, but she had something very important that gave her the smallest bit of hope—the location of the deed.

Sasha walked to a corner of the kitchen and crouched beside the warm oven, where she would be hidden and safe. "Well," she thought to herself, "I guess this is my new room now." She tried to make herself comfortable. Then she reached into her satchel, took out a pencil and her notebook, and began to write.

Dear Mama,

I am writing you from the Gentry mansion. Everything is so terrible. We miss you. Are you really in the middle of a war? I heard the Knights of Daytime are valorous, and each one is a storybook hero. Have you met Belfort the knight? Have you seen the Make Mad Order in person? What's it like? Do they really walk backward? We lost the house, but you know that already. I work for the Gentrys now, and Papa is a soup peddler. There are rumors that the Willow Wood has a roving beast like before. A wild boar, people say, but I think it might be Otto. We had to set him loose when we lost the house. We could use a hero too, you know.

Love,
Sasha

P.S. How do you know Puck?

CHAPTER 8

The next morning, Sasha was jolted awake by a splash of water in her face. Chef Barza stood above her, holding a now-empty pitcher.

"Wake up," said Barza.

Sasha rubbed her eyes.

"Now," said Barza, as she turned and walked to the counter. Sasha tried to get up and realized that her entire body was sore from curling up beside the pots and pans on the hard kitchen floor. She winced.

As soon as Sasha stood up, Barza shoved a

tray into her hands. It had Sisal's breakfast arranged on it. "Here," said Barza. The warm bread smelled so good that it made Sasha's knees buckle. She thought perhaps Barza would be nicer if she remembered how good a job Sasha had done.

"Did you like the kitchen?" she asked, hoping to remind her.

"Of course I like the kitchen," said Barza.

"I mean the cleanness."

"Yes."

"Okay. I just thought—I mean—it was spotless this morning."

"Yes," said Barza, annoyed. "That's what I told you to do—make it spotless."

"And it is."

"So then you've done what you were told. Do you need a parade for doing your job?"

"No," said Sasha.

"Everyone here does what they're told."

"I know. I just—"

"That's not something extra. You're not special for doing your job."

"Okay, I'm sorry," said Sasha. She wasn't expecting a parade, only some acknowledgment. Or at least the same respect that Barza seemed to give her cooks.

Sasha took the tray and started to walk out. "Wait," said Barza.

What now? thought Sasha. Would she scold her for holding the tray wrong?

"Take a roll on your way out." Barza nodded at a basket filled with glistening golden-brown butter bread. "I make them for my crew every morning," said Barza.

Sasha took a roll. It was still warm. She hadn't eaten anything for a day and a half. She took a bite. It was soft and fluffy and salty and buttery and perfect. All the aching in Sasha's bones seemed to disappear. It occurred to Sasha that Barza would have to wake up hours before her crew to make them breakfast. And that was so much extra work. She must have worked even harder to do it quietly as Sasha slept.

"Thank you," said Sasha with a mouthful of bread. Barza gave her a short nod. Sasha stuffed the roll into her mouth and took off toward the stairs.

Sasha made it up to the tower bedroom and entered just as Sisal was waking up. "Ah! Servant girl, you're on time this time."

Sasha set the tray beside Sisal's bed and started to walk out.

"Wait. What's this?" said Sisal.

"Your breakfast," said Sasha.

"No. Wrong. Water first. I mean, don't you want to slap your forehead and say you're a dum-dum bird?"

Sasha clenched her fists. She had to do it. She slapped her forehead and said, "I'm a dum-dum bird."

"But do you know *why* you're a dum-dum bird?" said Sisal.

"No," said Sasha.

"Because I need to wash my face first. Don't you want to get me water?"

"Yes, princess," said Sasha.

"Quickly," said Sisal.

Sasha rushed down the tower, got the water, then rushed back up. The whole time, she grumbled. But even though her future seemed like an endless loop of climbing up and down the tower steps, she wasn't hopeless anymore. She knew the location of the deed. All she needed next was a plan.

But plans weren't easy to come by. She needed

just a few minutes to think.

Sasha was out of breath as she poured the water into the basin in the washroom. She entered the bedroom and said, "It's ready."

Sisal had already begun eating her breakfast. She hopped out of bed and pranced to the washroom. As she left, she said, "Wouldn't you like to open the windows and dust everything and, I dunno, do servant things?"

Sasha reached into her satchel. She was tempted to throw the bottle of soup at Sisal. Instead, she grabbed a rag and began to draw back the curtains and dust the windowsills. At the last window, she heard a rustling sound. Sasha drew back the curtain.

"Ah!" Sasha jumped back in surprise. On the other side of the window, Puck was hanging upside down, looking in.

Puck laughed as Sasha composed herself and

hurried to open the window latch. "What are you doing hanging from a window? It's so good to see you! Did you contact Mama? Sisal will be back any second. You scared me!" All the thoughts were coming to her at once.

Puck was hanging like a monkey. He didn't seem at all bothered by the height. He reached out and said, "Guh!"

It was a "come here" grunt.

Sasha was in such a panic about Sisal returning that she took his hand. He pulled her toward him. "Oh no," she said.

"Gooby!"

Puck pulled, and Sasha was afraid that if she let go, he would fly backward and fall from the tower, so she climbed onto the sill. Then Puck helped her step onto the stone ledge outside. The wind was blowing softly. The morning sun was still gently warm. Puck had been hanging from the eaves above the window. He sat back up and guided Sasha up onto the roof of the tower.

Before she knew it, Sasha was sitting on the tallest peak of Gentry mansion, high in the air, above the Village, the King Sea, and the Willow Woods. The view was spectacular. She could see the Sparkstone Mountains glittering in the distance.

For a moment, it was magical.

And for the first time since losing her house, Sasha felt a restful calm.

"Puck," she said, "I know you can understand me."

"Guh," said Puck.

"But you can't quite talk."

"Guh."

"I always thought you were an ordinary forest baby, but just in case you're actually magic, I wanted to say thanks for looking out for me. You're my best friend."

Even though Puck's face was covered in dirt, Sasha could see a powerful blush. He looked down and smiled and then plowed into her for a hug. Sasha would have usually pulled away because she hated getting dirty, but she was already covered in sweat and grime. And she didn't care anyway. She would rather be with a dirt fairy like Puck than a spotless princess like Sisal.

Puck buried his face into her side and made a purring sound. She thought she heard him say, "You're welcome," but she must have been mistaken.

"What are you doing here, anyway?" said Sasha.

She knew that Sisal would be back from the washroom any minute. Puck reached into his tattered shirt and pulled out another soiled and crumpled letter. "Guh, guh!"

Was it a new letter from Mama? But Sasha hadn't even given hers to Puck yet. She unfolded the parchment and read:

Dear Sasha,

I heard the predicament from Prince Carvalio (who says you call him Puck. That's funny. He must like you).

Sasha paused her reading to say, "Wait. You can talk?"

"Yuh huh, gooby," said Puck, nudging her back to the letter.

Sasha let it go and kept reading:

I believe in you. You can get the deed back. I know it. I've sent three potions to help you form a plan. One is to create a distraction. One is to give you light in the darkness. And one is to make you invincible with superstrength—it tastes like cherries. I know you will use them well, my darling girl.   *All my love,*

Maxima Bebbin

Sasha was so relieved that she laughed aloud as she tucked the letter into her pocket. Mama had saved the day, especially with the superpower potion. She said, "Of all the odds and oddity, Mama did it. She saved us. Now, where are the potions?"

Puck rooted around in his shirt and pulled out two glass vials. One was labeled DISTRACTION, and the other ANTI-DARK. He handed them over.

"Great," said Sasha, "but what about the superpower one?"

Puck suddenly became bashful.

"You didn't," said Sasha.

Puck let out a burp.

It smelled like cherries.

"How dare you," said Sasha. "I take back everything I said. You're a wicked monkey. You're a wastrel. You're disobedient and unreliable."

Puck giggled and gave her a salute. "Tantu!" he said. He knew she wasn't serious. Then he fell backward off the roof.

Sasha rushed to the edge in time to see him falling backward through the trees. At the last possible second, he twisted his body and landed on all fours like a squirrel.

Either the superpower potion had protected him, or Puck was some kind of mud-covered stray cat. Sasha didn't know what to believe anymore.

Puck waved to her from below then scampered off. Sasha could see the guard dog, Abrus, barking and chasing after him, but Puck was too tricksy and quick. He scurried through the gardens and bounded over the wall as the dog gnashed at his heels.

Sasha took one last look at the valley. Even without the third potion, she had everything she needed for a plan. She took a deep breath and thought, *By golly, this just might work.*

When Sasha climbed down to the window ledge and back into the tower, Sisal was waiting with her arms crossed and a furious scowl. "Where have you been?"

Crumbsy bumsy, thought Sasha. *This will never work.*

CHAPTER 9

Sisal was not pleased.

Even though she assumed that Sasha was cleaning the roof because the persuasion potion had worked too well, she wanted her servant girl available at *all times*. She punished Sasha by suggesting that she clean the entire tower, scrub three loads of laundry, complete all of Sisal's schoolwork, and polish all her shoes.

It took all morning.

Sisal stayed in bed and read her favorite picture books the entire time. When the bells finally rang for family teatime, Sasha's hands were blistered from all the scrubbing. "Come now, servant girl," said Sisal. "I think you'd love to watch me eat rice pudding, wouldn't you?"

"Sure," said Sasha. She only had to survive until that night. Her plan was simple:

1. Wait until everyone was asleep, even the baron.
2. Sneak into the dungeon office.
3. Grab the deed from behind the painting.
4. Drink the antidote to the persuasion potion in front of Sisal so that she would think Sasha was free of the spell (even though there was never any spell).
5. Escape through the back door of the kitchens.
6. Give the rest of the antidote to Papa, so he would stop thinking he was under the spell.
7. Move back into the *Juicy Gizzard* and save Papa from soup peddling and write letters to Mama and be happy forever.

Simple.

But when Sasha took her place next to Barza along the wall, she got the worst possible news. The baron Vadim Gentry was pouring wax onto a folded letter. Then he placed his ring in the hot wax to create a seal. As he waited for the wax to cool, he waved Butta over. "Butta," he said, "I want you to go to my office..."

Butta whispered something that Sasha couldn't hear.

"No, the other one," said the baron. "To the special shelf, and get the papers."

Sasha stepped forward to hear better, but a heavy, familiar hand clamped on her shoulder. It was Barza, pulling her back to her position by the wall.

Sasha strained to hear, but all she caught was, "Put them on the first caravan to my safe in the Rozny bank. I want that deed locked away forever."

Butta nodded and turned to go execute the order.

In that moment, Sasha knew that her plan was doomed to fail, since the baron was going to ship the deed to Rozny before nightfall, and even if she could change her plan, Sasha had two terrible obstacles, Barza and Butta.

Sasha looked around for ideas.

Sisal was greedily stuffing rice pudding into her mouth.

Her mother, Rose, sat with her glass of tea, sipping it peacefully.

Sasha felt all hope slipping through her fingers until she made eye contact with Mrs. Gentry. When Rose saw her—panicked at the thought of Butta shipping the deed to Rozny—she put down her tea and said, "Butta, before you leave, could you please attend to me?"

Butta was already at the door, but he

turned back.

"I'd like a bowl of pomegranate," said Mrs. Gentry. "Would you peel one for me?" Butta nodded and began the slow process of plucking the seeds from a pomegranate. Mrs. Gentry took another sip of her tea and gave Sasha a mischievous wink.

That left Barza.

Sasha was imagining a sudden move to lunge

away from Barza's grip. But right then, she heard the chef whisper, "Go. You've been a good worker, and I hate to lose you. But go."

Sasha felt Barza's hand lift from her shoulder.

She had finally won the chef's respect. Sasha was overwhelmed with pride. But she didn't have time to bask in her accomplishment. She reached into her satchel, took out the potion labeled, DISTRACTION, and popped the cork.

The bottle began to whistle and fizz immediately. Sasha rolled the bottle across the floor, toward the middle of the room, just as a massive purple cloud burst and swirled out of it, filling the entire parlor.

The servants ran to open the windows. Baron Gentry shouted, "What is the meaning of this?"

For a moment, it was chaos.

Sasha ran to the door and slipped out before

anyone noticed.

As she ran down the hall, she could hear Sisal shouting, "Girl! Girl, get over here and fan me. Girl!"

But Sasha didn't waste a second. She sprinted to the stairs that led down to the kitchens. Then she descended again to the dungeon floor.

But that was as far as she got.

The second basement was so far underground that it was completely dark, even in the daytime. And this time, the baron's office wasn't lit up. Sasha found herself in blackness so thick that she lost all sense of direction.

She spun around but couldn't see the stairs anymore.

Sasha was lost.

She put her hands out to protect herself from walking into anything, but she couldn't even see her hands.

Sasha was afraid.

Any moment, the distraction potion would fade, and Butta would come down with a torch and catch her. Sasha reached into her satchel and felt around until she found the potion from Mama that would have read ANTI-DARK, if she could see it.

She held it as far away from herself as possible. If it was anything like the distraction potion, it would probably shoot fireworks all over the place.

Sasha winced as she popped the cork. The thin vial of glass began to glow as gently as a firefly. "Thank you," said Sasha as a warm globe of light surrounded her and showed her the way through the long hall. Sasha rushed to the office door and pushed it open.

She was almost there.

All she had to do was—

Sasha stopped in her tracks when she heard the sound of a dog's growl.

Abrus the guard dog stepped into the light.

He had been sleeping on the carpet in front of the baron's desk. "Easy," said Sasha, taking a step back. Abrus bared his teeth and growled again. He knew that this was his master's secret office. No one else was allowed.

Sasha was nearly frozen with fear. *Crumbsy bumsy*, she thought. If only she had that superpower potion. Mama really had thought of everything. Facing the angry dog without the potion seemed like a terrible idea. Even though she *still* didn't believe in magic, at least it would give her a little confidence, or the smell would distract Abrus or something...

Right then, Sasha remembered something even better than magic.

Soup.

Papa's bottle of bone soup. She reached into her satchel and pulled out the very not-magic potion. Abrus barked as soon as she moved. Sasha flinched. "It's okay," she said. "It's okay. Here." She opened the bottle and poured the soup onto the stone floor. Abrus's ears went back as his snout filled with the aroma of soup. He bounced over and began to lick it up.

Sasha breathed a sigh of relief and stepped aside to let the big dog enjoy the tasty puddle. She walked over to the painting of Rose Gentry and pulled it aside. She stuffed the deed and the vial into her satchel, then tiptoed back across Abrus's path and into the dark hall once again.

Sasha ran up the stairs, through the kitchens that had been her bedroom, and to the back door. But when she was just about to open the door, she heard a familiar voice.

"What are you doing, girl? How dare you?"

It was Sisal.

Sasha turned slowly.

Sisal stood in the kitchens with her hands on her hips. "Are you running away? I called for you, like, a thousand times. I want more strawberries. But you were sneaking around."

"I'm leaving," said Sasha.

"No, you're not."

"I have the persuasion cure," said Sasha.

"But you're a fool, and you didn't drink it yet," said Sisal. "Now, come here."

Sasha walked over.

"Get the potion," said Sisal.

Sasha reached into her satchel and took out the bottle.

"Open it," said Sisal.

Sasha popped off the cork.

"Now," said Sisal, "you're going to be my servant forever. Pour it out."

Sasha didn't.

"I said, pour it out."

"There's just one thing," said Sasha.

"Pour it out!" said Sisal. "Now!"

"You didn't ask in the form of a suggestion."

Sisal's eyes went wide as she realized her mistake. Before she could say anything, Sasha took a big gulp from the vial. "No!" cried Sisal.

Sasha shrugged and put the cork back in the vial. She would need the other half of the antidote for Papa. Sasha turned and walked out the door. She didn't have anything more to say to Sisal. She only wanted to taste the fresh air of springtime in the valley as she ran down the hill toward the Village.

She was free.

Her heart felt featherlight.

It was lifted with the hope of a better future.

Papa could stop peddling soup.

They had a home again.

Mama was safe.

And Puck was maybe magic—but also her best friend.

Sasha laughed as she ran to the village market and felt her worries fall far, far behind.

CHAPTER 10

Dear Mama,

We did it! We got the house back. Papa was so happy when he heard the news, he threw Puck into the air and caught him a bunch of times. Papa can cook a really good bone soup now. You've got to try it. He says he'll make lesser potions for now, and things can be calm for a while.

We had to spend half the money we got from the persuasion potion on a hedge knight army to go into the Willow Wood and fetch

Otto. He caused a lot of trouble. Then the constable came by, and we returned the rest of the coins to the baron and showed our deed, and everything was back to normal. The constable said the baron wanted to hire his own soldiers to come take our deed, but

Rose forbid it. You two must have been good friends.

Thank you for the potions. I hope you come back soon.

Love, Sasha

P.S. I'm starting to think Puck is magic.

DANIEL NAYERI was born in Iran and spent a couple of years as a refugee before immigrating to Oklahoma at the age of eight with his family. He is the author of several books for young readers, including *Straw House, Wood House, Brick House, Blow.*

ESTRELA LOURENÇO was born in Lisbon, where she later studied animation. She moved to Ireland in 2009 and has since worked as an animator, animation director, and episodic director. She is currently storyboard revisionist for Hasbro. Past clients include Disney Television and Cartoon Network. As a freelancer, she works in comics and illustration.